Postman Pat

The Difficult Day

Story by **John Cunliffe**
Pictures by **Celia Berridge**

from the original Television designs by Ivor Wood

Scholastic Children's Books,
Commonwealth House, 1 – 19 New Oxford Street, London WC1A 1NU
A division of Scholastic Limited
London – New York – Toronto – Sydney – Auckland

First published by in hardback by André Deutsch Limited, 1982

This edition published by Scholastic Limited, 1996

Text copyright © John Cunliffe, 1982
Illustrations copyright © Celia Berridge and
Woodland Animations Limited, 1982

ISBN 0 590 13435 3

Printed in Italy by Amadeus S.p.A. – Rome

10 9 8 7 6 5 4 3 2

The right of John Cunliffe, Celia Berridge and Ivor Wood to be
identified as the author and illustrators of this work has been asserted
by them in accordance with the Copyright, Designs and Patents Act, 1988.

It was a lovely morning in Greendale. The sun was shining. The birds were singing. Where was Postman Pat? It was long past his time to be up and on his way, but his curtains were closed and his van stood outside. All was silent and still. Then...the door opened and Pat looked out. He looked sleepily at his watch. "Oh dear, is it *that* time?"

He dressed and rushed out without any breakfast, and without his hat!
He dashed back for his hat, fell over his cat, and landed in a heap on
the doorstep.

He picked up Jess and ran to his van, saying, "Come on, let's get moving, Jess. We're ever so late."

He talked to Jess as they drove along the winding roads.

"What a start to the day! I wonder why that blooming alarm clock didn't go off. We'll have to see if Ted can mend it."

Mrs Goggins was having a difficult morning, too. She was trying to mend a parcel. It was for Ted Glen. When Pat arrived he tried to help, but they got all tangled up in sticky tape! What a muddle!

"I do wish people would wrap parcels up properly," said Mrs Goggins. "This is in a right old mess – and heavy, too. I don't know what Ted will say."

"It's just one of those days," said Pat. "First I slept in, because my alarm didn't go off, then this parcel. Never mind, it's a lovely morning. Cheerio!"

Pat was on his way. He saw Ted, mending a fence on the hillside.

"Hello," he said, "there's Ted. I'll give him his parcel before it falls to bits."

He stopped and shouted to Ted, "Hi! Ted – there's a parcel for you."

Ted came down the hill. Pat passed the parcel to him over the wall. He was just saying, "Be careful, Ted, it's a bit loose," when...

"Oooooops!" It slipped, and Ted dropped it.

"Oh, *no!*"

Dozens of little balls, and wheels, and screws, rolled away into the grass. Ted, on his hands and knees, began to scratch and search for them.

"Nay," he said, "I'll never find them in all this long grass."

"Hold on," said Pat, climbing over the wall, "I'll give you a hand."

"It's hopeless," said Ted.

When Bill Thompson saw them, he came over to see what they were doing.

"I have just the thing," he said. It was a large magnet. It picked up all the wheels, and balls, and screws from the grass.

"I hope they're all there," said Pat.

"I'll count them," said Ted. "Thanks."

"Cheerio Ted."

"Cheerio Pat."

Ted said, "Thanks," to Bill; "that was real handy."

Pat's next stop was at Thompson Ground. Alf was up a ladder, mending the barn wall. Pat was just walking under the ladder when Alf shouted, "Look out!"
Too late!

"Oooooooohhhh! Ouch!" said Pat.

Alf had dropped his tin of nails. Pat tried to catch it – twisted round – lost his balance – and sat down with a bump, with his hand twisted under him. Alf came down the ladder.

"You all right, Pat?"

"No, I think I've sprained my wrist."

"I'll go and get a bandage," said Alf.

Then Mrs Thompson came along.

"Dear me, whatever have you been up to, Pat?"

"Just in too much of a hurry," said Pat. "Walking under ladders."

Mrs Thompson looked at his wrist. "Now hold still," he said, "and I'll bind it up for you. But you won't be able to drive any more today, you know. You'll have to rest it."

"What about all my letters?" said Pat.

Sam Waldron arrived in his mobile shop. They told him about Pat's accident.

"Why don't you put your letters and parcels in my van?" said Sam. "We can do our rounds together."

"And the post will get through after all," said Pat. "Thanks, Sam; it's a grand idea."

Everyone helped to move the parcels and letters into Sam's van.

"There's plenty of room," said Sam. "Just stack them at the back of the van behind the seats."

"Come on, Jess," said Mrs Thompson. She put Jess on the seat. "You'll be all right in there."

Pat climbed in beside Sam, and Jess curled up on his knee.

"Off we go," said Sam.

Away they went.

"What a surprise everyone will get, when they see us together," said Pat.

And so they did.

Pat's hand was still hurting, so they made their first stop at Dr Gilbertson's house. She had a good look at his hand, and said, "It's not broken. You'll be all right in a day or two. I'll just give you something to soothe it."
She gave him a jar of cream that took the pain away.

"Thank you, doctor," said Pat. "Cheerio!"

On they went to Greendale Farm.

"What a good idea," said Mrs Pottage, when she saw them. "We can get our post and parcels with our potatoes and peas."

All the people of Greendale agreed with her, as Pat and Sam went on their way. The Reverend Timms...Miss Hubbard...Granny Dryden...George Lancaster...Peter Fogg...and all the children.

Jess liked Sam's van, too, because the smell of fish tickled his nose. At the end of the day, Sam gave Jess a kipper all to himself, and that turned a difficult day into a perfect day, as far as Jess was concerned.